Plants and Animals

Written by
Stephen Rickard

Trees are plants.
They need air and water.

Cats are animals.
They need air and water too.

Ants are animals.
They need air and water.

Peppers are plants.
They need air and water too.

Sunflowers are plants.
They need air and water.

Frogs are animals.
They need air and water too.

Snakes are animals.
They need air and water.

Carrots are plants.
They need air and water too.

Poppies are plants.
They need air and water.

People are animals.
We need air and water too.

Plants	**Animals**
trees	cats
peppers	ants
sunflowers	frogs
carrots	snakes
poppies	people